To
Highland Baptist Church

Ima & The Great Texas Ostrich Race

Happy Reading
and Racing!

Margaret McManis

Words by Margaret McManis   Pictures by Bruce Dupree

EAKIN PRESS ✦ Austin, Texas

FIRST EDITION
Text Copyright © 2002 by Margaret McManis
Illustrations Copyright © 2002 by Bruce Dupree
Published in the United States of America
By Eakin Press/A Division of Sunbelt Media, Inc.
P.O. Drawer 90159 ✦ Austin, Texas 78709-0159
email: sales@eakinpress.com
💻 website: www.eakinpress.com 💻
ALL RIGHTS RESERVED.
Printed in Hong Kong
2 3 4 5 6 7 8 9
ISBN 1-57168-605-3 HB
1-57168-671-1 PB

Library of Congress Cataloging-in-Publication Data

McManis, Margaret Olivia.
  Ima & the great Texas ostrich race / words by Margaret McManis; pictures by Bruce Dupree.
    p. cm.
  Summary: In 1892 on a Texas ranch, ten-year-old Ima Hogg rides her pet ostrich in a race against her brothers who are on horseback. Includes facts about the real Ima, daughter of Texas Governor James Stephen Hogg.
    ISBN 1-57168-605-3 – ISBN 1-57168-671-1 (pbk : alk. paper)
  1. Hogg, Ima–Juvenile fiction. [1. Hogg, Ima–Fiction. 2. Ostriches–Fiction. 3. Racing–Fiction. 4. Brothers and sisters–Fiction. 5. Texas–History–1846-1950–Fiction.] I. Title: Ima and the great Texas ostrich race. II. Dupree, Bruce, ill. III. Title.
PZ7.M4856 Im 2002
[Fic]–dc21   2002004949

Papa told me not to brag too much. I promised I wouldn't. Papa says a real lady knows her own worth and doesn't have to tell everyone. People listen to Papa all over the state of Texas.

I listen too… most times.

But I didn't when the Union Pacific locomotive lumbered into the station on my tenth birthday. Papa pointed to the last car on the line.

"Happy birthday, Ima!" he hollered as two men lowered a yellow ramp from the side of the caboose.

I stood at the end of the ramp, my feet hopping with curiosity. Even my toes were curious. "What is it? What *is* it, Papa?" I jumped with anticipation.

The wobbly ramp hit the ground with a crash, and out raced the biggest, ugliest bird thing I had ever seen. And boy, could that thing run! It headed down Main Street, black and white feathers flapping, and long legs stirring up a trail of dust. That crazy-looking bird thing outran every last one of Papa's wranglers! By the time the boys rounded him up to put him in a cage, my mind had already hatched a mighty fine plan.

"Governor Hogg, that there bird thing just ain't natural, sir," coughed a tired wrangler as he slid the bolt shut on the cage.

Papa just laughed. "Ima, girl, you got yourself one fast bird... I mean ostrich."

I smiled back at Papa and hugged his round body. An ostrich was something I hadn't reckoned on. What would my brothers think of my bird, my Ossy?

Will whooped with laughter at the sight of Ossy. "Why, little sister, that's the silliest-looking bird in the whole state of Texas!"

Brother Tom joined in. "*He-he-he-he-haw,* wh-why, Ima, that ole bird can't even fly! And would you take a gander at those drumsticks?" he bellowed.

I sort of broke my no-bragging promise to Papa when I shouted, "Ossy may be silly looking, but he's the fastest racing bird in all of Texas!"

"*Pshaw!* Fast he may be, but who ever heard of an ostrich that could race?" Will snickered. "Anyway, who's gonna saddle that ornery-looking thing?"

"And I don't see no teeth in that mouth of his. What about a bridle?" Tom roared.

My feet were not curious now, not curious at all! They were mad. Even my toes were mad!

"I'll ride Ossy, and beat both of you! I'll show you!" I shouted as I stamped off, my feet stirring up a storm of Texas dust.

The next morning a wrangler helped me up to Ossy's tall, black-and-white-feathered back. Papa handed me the reins.

"Hang on, Ima!" he shouted as he released the bird.

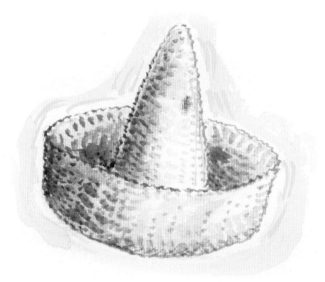

Boy, could that bird buck! He whirled his slender brown neck around like a wrangler lassoing a heifer. His big eyes rolled back and forth, and he hissed like a rock rattler. I flew over the top of the corral and buried my face in the hard, dry sand.

"Hold him, Papa, hold him!" I cried. I scrambled under the fence, wiped the dirt from my eyes, and took the reins once more. Ossy blinked in my direction. He leaped into the air. Then he flapped his enormous wings and ran in circles while hissing mightily.

This time I stayed put like sorghum syrup.

"Why, Ima!" Papa shouted proudly. "Girl, you've got mettle!"

A great race was planned for the next day, and news of it spread like a West Texas prairie fire.

"Hey, little sister, are you and that overstuffed turkey thinking about winning this race?" Will hooted from the back of his horse.

Tom snickered at my bird. "Gobble, gobble!" he mocked.

"Now, Ima girl, don't let those boys hornswoggle ya," encouraged Papa. "You're the best—and I'm not bragging!"

Papa could always make me feel better, even when I was down real low.

The next morning Tom and Will grinned at me from the starting line. They had the best quarter horses money could buy, but there was something they didn't have. A thing Papa told me that I have—METTLE!

When the gun sounded, their horses raced forward. Ossy leaped wildly into the air. His big eyes rolled from side to side and his neck swung around. He ran in circles. I tried to remember what Papa had said: *Show him your mettle, Ima!* I pulled on the reins firmly and talked to Ossy soothingly.

The wind snapped my hair around as the brush-covered hills whooshed past. Tom and Will were far ahead, their horses' hooves stirring up the dusty road. Ossy pumped his gigantic drumsticks and sped ahead. I smelled the sweat of Tom's gelding as we streaked past. My brother's eyes nearly popped out of his head.

"Gobble, gobble, big brother!" I shouted.

Now brother Will turned his head and glanced back in my direction. I rounded the last corner and saw Papa standing by a sorghum barrel that marked the finish line. His grin was as wide as the Brazos River. Will stared in disbelief at the strange bird coming alongside his prize-winning horse. The pounding of hooves and claws filled my ears. Dirt clogged my throat and eyes, but mettle filled my heart.

Ossy's gait was smooth as buttermilk. His four enormous claws pulled at the hard-packed dirt. I pressed my knees into his feathered sides, and Ossy slowly pulled ahead.

Now it was *my* turn to look back and smile at my brother. It felt good! I watched him wipe grit and dust from his tight mouth. His horse would not give up so easily. To be defeated by a bird was no joke to him either!

Then Ossy stuck out his long neck and streaked past that sorghum barrel. We were only one inch ahead!

The whole state seemed to be sitting on Papa's corral fence that day, watching in amazement as my Ossy came roaring across the finish line, black and white feathers and long legs stirring up a curious Texas dust storm.

Papa looked up into my smiling, dirt-covered face and winked. I knew for sure the worth of a real lady—especially a lady with lots of mettle. I decided to keep my promise to Papa, and didn't brag once about winning.

People listen to Papa all over the state of Texas. After all, he *is* the governor. I listen, too, and it sure feels good!

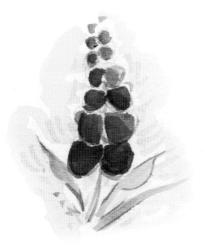

Was there really a girl named
Ima Hogg?

Yes, there really was an Ima Hogg, and what a life she led! The only daughter of Governor James Stephen Hogg of Texas, Ima enjoyed a wonderful childhood filled with exciting adventures. She was eight when her father was elected governor in 1890, and their home was filled with famous people and exotic animals, including two ostriches named Jack and Jill. Ima's brothers really did dare her to ride one of the ostriches, but as soon as she sat upon it, Tom shot it with a pea shooter and Ima was bucked off!

Called "Miss Ima" by everyone who knew her, Ima Hogg lived a long and fruitful life (1882-1975). She visited cities all over the world while studying to become a concert pianist. Later, while living in Houston, Texas, she became widely known for her work in philanthropy (which means offering time, money, and interest to help improve the lives of others). Miss Ima accomplished much in supporting the arts, historical preservation, and mental health programs.

Oh, and to set the record straight about the legend of Ima's sister Ura, the author has this to say: "Yes, there was an Ima Hogg, but Ura Hogg was pure Hoggwash!"

www.imahogg.net

In loving memory of Kenneth Eugene Marsh and John Edward Marsh II, our Marshmallow Men.

Is there really a
Margaret Olivia McManis?

Yes, the author of this book, Margaret McManis, lives in Lake Jackson, Texas. Ms. McManis has had a long career with books. She first became a "Book Boss" as a library assistant at

Sweeny High School, and then followed her dreams of becoming a librarian and an author. Along the way she has learned about fascinating characters in Texas history. Since she lives near Varner-Hogg Plantation in West Columbia, Texas, the author has learned a lot about "Miss Ima." Through her books based on the young life of Ima, Ms. McManis hopes to introduce kids to this great lady of Texas.

What about Bruce Dupree?

Bruce Dupree is an artist and professor at Auburn University. Mr. Dupree has won numerous regional and national awards for graphic design and illustration. Books he has authored and/or illustrated include: *Ima and the Great Texas Ostrich Race, Hernando De Soto, Coming Home Auburn!, Homecoming Alabama!, The Golden Horse,* and *The Golden Horse-The Journey West.*